It's the day of the Cupcake Bake, and
Dr KittyCat and Peanut are judges! But
when Mrs Hazelnut meets them outside
the baking marquee she looks worried.
What can be happening inside? You'll
have to read the story to find out!

For Minerva (Minnie)
the cat. J.C.

# OXFORD
UNIVERSITY PRESS

Great Clarendon Street, Oxford OX2 6DP
Oxford University Press is a department of the University of Oxford.
It furthers the University's objective of excellence in research, scholarship,
and education by publishing worldwide

Cover artwork: Richard Byrne
Cover photographs: Tony Campbell, Kuttelvaserova Stuchelova,
Bartkowski /Shutterstock.com
Inside artwork: Dynamo
All animal images from Shutterstock
With thanks to Christopher Tancock for advising on the first aid

First published in 2015

British Library Cataloguing in Publication Data

Data available

ISBN: 978-0-19-274333-6 (paperback)

2 4 6 8 10 9 7 5 3 1

Printed in Great Britain
Paper used in the production of this book is a natural,
recyclable product made from wood grown in sustainable forests.
The manufacturing process conforms to the environmental
regulations of the country of origin.

Are you crazy about your pet?

Do you love cute and cuddly animals?

For budding doctors and nurses!

Perfect for fans of Holly Webb.

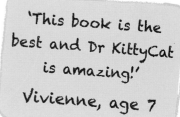

'I like Dr KittyCat's helper because
I like helping too, and his name is
funny because he's called Peanut!'
Frankie, age 5

'I think that the pictures are clever as
they're real animals on pretend bodies.'
Harriet, age 7

# A note from the author:

## Jane says . . .

'Our kitten, Minnie, liked to
lie on her back on the floor
and claw her way under the
sofa and out the other side.
One day she didn't
come out. She'd
shredded the
material so badly
she'd got caught
up in it and needed
to be cut out!'

**Dr KittyCat**

is ready to rescue

# Daisy the Kitten

## Jane Clarke

OXFORD
UNIVERSITY PRESS

# Chapter One

Peanut the mouse wheeled a dentist's chair into the middle of Dr KittyCat's clinic.

'There's a lot to do on Shiny Smiles day,' he squeaked as he pulled a folding screen around the chair. 'And it's the Thistletown Festival, too. Don't forget we're judging the Cupcake Bake at three o'clock.'

'I can't wait to taste everyone's cupcakes!' Dr KittyCat meowed. She laid out a row of long, thin, shiny instruments on her desk.

'Dental mirrors, tweezers, probes, scalers . . .' she murmured. 'We're ready to go.'

Peanut scampered across to the door and opened it. A line of little animals was waiting outside.

'Come in, everyone,' he told them. 'Dr KittyCat's ready to check your shiny smiles.' Peanut opened a notebook that said 'Furry First-aid Book' on the front cover. It was where Dr KittyCat kept her medical and dental notes about all the little animals in Thistletown. 'Who's first?' he asked.

A small hedgehog stepped forward. His ears were twitching nervously.

'I am,' he whispered.

'Follow me . . .' Peanut led him behind the screen.

The hedgehog gave a little squeal when he saw the dentist's chair.

'There's no need to worry,'
Dr KittyCat meowed. 'You're safe
in our paws.'

Peanut opened Dr KittyCat's *Furry
First-aid Book* and flipped through it.
'It's the first time that Bramble has been
to Shiny Smiles,' he told Dr KittyCat, as
the young hedgehog scrambled onto the
dentist's chair.

'All you have to do is open your
mouth wide,' Peanut instructed, tucking
a cape carefully under Bramble's chin.
Bramble took one look at the

row of shiny dental instruments and clamped his jaws shut. His whiskers began to quiver.

'You need to open your mouth now,' Peanut told him gently.

Bramble shook his head and curled up into a prickly ball.

'How can we check Bramble's teeth now?' Peanut squeaked worriedly.

'Don't panic, Peanut,' Dr KittyCat meowed calmly. 'It takes some little animals a while to get used to the idea of coming to our Shiny Smiles clinic and having their mouths examined regularly. We don't want to rush things and scare them away.' She turned to the little hedgehog.

'It doesn't matter if it takes more than one visit for you to have your teeth checked, Bramble,' she reassured him. 'It's not an emergency. You don't have to open your mouth if you don't want to.'

Bramble slowly uncurled himself and poked out his nose.

Peanut was glad to see that his whiskers had stopped quivering. Bramble smiled a tiny smile that showed a glimpse of his front teeth.

Dr KittyCat turned to her
row of dental instruments and picked
up a little mirror on a long, thin
handle. She held it up to the nervous
little hedgehog.

'You have very nice teeth,' she purred, 'and we want to keep them that way. Next time, do you think you could open your jaws wide enough for me to put this dental mirror in your mouth so I can do a proper check?'

'Yes!' Bramble promised. He scampered down from the chair. 'Do I still get a sticker?' he asked anxiously.

'Of course,' Dr KittyCat purred. She handed him a sticker which said: 'I was a purr-fect patient for Dr KittyCat!'

I was a purr-fect patient for Dr KittyCat!

Peanut poked his head round the screen.

'Next!' he called.

A very small and fluffy kitten sprang up onto the dentist's chair and opened her mouth wide, showing all her sharp little baby teeth. Peanut checked his notebook.

'This is Daisy's second visit to our Shiny Smiles clinic, so she knows what to do,' he chuckled.

Peanut passed Dr KittyCat the sterilized mirror and she carefully examined every surface of each one of Daisy's teeth. Then she took a long, thin instrument with a hook on the end and very gently probed between each tooth.

'Daisy, your teeth are purr-fect. You can rinse out, now,' Dr KittyCat smiled. 'Your mouth is very healthy. It won't be long before you get your grown-up teeth. One of your teeth has just started to wobble and it will fall out soon,' she went on. 'Your new teeth will be a lot bigger, especially the long, pointy ones on the side. They're called canines.'

'Your grown-up teeth will look like Dr KittyCat's,' Peanut told her.

'That's good because when I grow up I want to be just like Dr KittyCat,'

Daisy giggled as she took her sticker and jumped down from the chair.

'Nutmeg!' Daisy called. 'It's your turn now. I'll wait for you.'

A young guinea pig hopped up onto the dentist's chair.

'My gum is sore,' Nutmeg told Dr KittyCat. 'It feels as if something's stuck in it.'

'We'll soon sort that out,' Dr KittyCat reassured her. She tucked the cape under Nutmeg's chin and picked out a long, thin pair of tweezers.

'A seed was stuck between your teeth and your gum,' Dr KittyCat exclaimed, holding it up for Nutmeg to see. 'You must have missed it when you brushed your teeth. Peanut will show you how to brush them properly.'

Peanut took a toothbrush. 'Don't just go up and down—go round and

round in tiny circles like this,' he said as he demonstrated the actions.

'It's important that everyone brushes their teeth very carefully every day,' Dr KittyCat told Nutmeg.

'Especially today,' Peanut laughed. He handed Nutmeg her sticker. 'Everyone will be eating sweet things this afternoon at the Cupcake Bake.'

'Did you know that anyone who enters has to make six cupcakes?' Nutmeg told them excitedly as she jumped down from the chair. 'I'm making seedy cupcakes with cherries on the top.'

'Yummy!' Peanut murmured.

'I'm going to make sticky toffee cupcakes with swirly buttercream icing,' Daisy meowed from the other side of the screen.

'Delicious,' Dr KittyCat purred.

'I'm going to use lots of sprinkles,' Posy the puppy piped up.

'And I'm putting smiley faces on mine,' Fennel the fox cub yipped.

Peanut stuck his head round the screen.

'I can't wait to taste all of your cupcakes!' he squeaked. 'Now, let's see—Fennel, are you next?'

By lunchtime, all the little animals'
teeth had been checked. Peanut began
to sterilize the dental instruments
that Dr KittyCat had used and put
them away.

'Will you need any of these things
before the next Shiny Smiles day?'
he asked.

Dr KittyCat opened her flowery
doctor's bag and checked the
contents. 'Scissors, syringe,
medicines, ointments, instant
cool packs, paw-cleansing
gel, mouth gel, wipes.
Stethoscope, ophthalmoscope,
ear thermometer, tweezers,

bandages, gauze, sticking plasters, peppermint lozenges, reward stickers, my knitting… That long, thin dental mirror would be a good thing to add to my bag,' she told Peanut. 'It's very useful for examining patients' mouths. And I think we should take the surgical headlamp, too.'

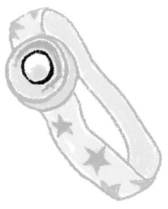

Peanut handed it to her, just as the old fashioned telephone on the desk began to ring.

Peanut scampered towards the phone—but before he could answer it, Dr KittyCat stretched out a paw and picked up the handset. She pricked up her furry ears

Brring!
Brring!

and listened carefully to the call. Peanut's heart began to thump. Who needed their help this time?

'We'll be there in a whisker!'
Dr KittyCat meowed. She grabbed
her flowery doctor's bag.

'It's Daisy!' Dr KittyCat told
Peanut. 'She's hurt herself at the
Cupcake Bake. So we're needed there
earlier than we thought!'

# Chapter Two

'Poor little Daisy,' Peanut squeaked. 'I hope she's not badly hurt!' He picked up the *Furry First-aid Book* and hurried after Dr KittyCat.

The vanbulance was parked in its usual place next to the clinic. Peanut pulled open the flowery door, leaped onto the passenger seat and tucked in his tail.

Dr KittyCat threw her flowery doctor's bag onto the front seat next to him and jumped up beside it. She checked her stripy tail was out of the way and closed the door. Peanut glanced over to her as they both clicked on their seatbelts.

'Ready to rescue?' Dr KittyCat meowed. She grabbed hold of the steering wheel and started the engine.

'Ready to rescue!' Peanut squeaked. He hit the button on the dashboard to make the siren light flash.

Nee-nah! Nee-nah! Nee-nah! The vanbulance sped off through Thistletown.

Peanut clutched at the dashboard as the vanbulance bumped and rumbled over the timber bridge. The tyres squealed as they rounded Duckpond Bend and raced along the country lane. Peanut stifled an anxious squeak and tried to stop his whiskers quivering. *Don't panic, Peanut,* he told himself, *Dr KittyCat drives fast, but she always drives safely.*

In no time at all they were at
the meadow. With a *scr-ee-eech* of
the brakes, Dr KittyCat brought the
vanbulance to a halt next to a big,
bright banner that said, 'Welcome to
Thistletown Festival!' Peanut sighed
with relief as he turned off the siren
and jumped out.

The festival field was crammed full
of brightly coloured tents and tepees.

Peanut read the signs. 'Storytelling, coil pot making, music, dancing, knitting . . . Something different's going on in every tent,' he squeaked. 'Where's the Cupcake Bake taking place?'

Dr KittyCat pointed to a large canvas tent at the far end of the field. Two flags, each with a picture of a cupcake, and a string of colourful bunting fluttered in the breeze above the tent.

'In that marquee,' Dr KittyCat said, leading the way towards it. 'So that's where Daisy must be . . .'

Mrs Hazelnut greeted them at the entrance. 'Thank goodness you've arrived,' she said.

Inside the marquee, a group of little animals wearing aprons and chefs' hats was gathered around what looked like a small and very fluffy ball of fur. It was Daisy. The tiny kitten was curled up on the wooden floor beside one of the cookery counters. She was crying as if her heart would break.

Dr KittyCat and Peanut made a beeline towards her. Dr KittyCat set down her flowery doctor's bag next to the fluffy kitten.

'We're here now, Daisy,' she purred. 'Tell us what's wrong.'

Daisy's nose was covered in flour and tears were rolling down her fluffy cheeks. She waved a tiny paw at the flour-speckled counter. Seven tiny cupcakes were sitting on a cooling rack in the middle of a sticky jumble of mixing bowls, spoons, and baking tins.

'I need to put icing on my cakes,'
Daisy wailed. 'But I can't do it. It hurts
too much!'

'We'll make you better as soon as
we find out what the matter is,'
Dr KittyCat reassured her.

Dr KittyCat smiled up at
Mrs Hazelnut and the little animals.
'Daisy is safe in our paws,' she told
them. 'Please get on with making your
cupcakes while we help her.'

Peanut turned to Daisy. 'Now,
Daisy,' he squeaked. 'You told us about
your cupcakes, but what Dr KittyCat
really needs to know is exactly what
part of you is hurting . . .'

# Chapter Three

The tiny kitten looked up at Peanut and Dr KittyCat and blinked her tear-filled eyes.

'It's my mouth,' she sobbed. 'It's very sore.'

'Your mouth?' Peanut squeaked. 'Your mouth was fine a couple of hours ago at our Shiny Smiles clinic.

Dr KittyCat even said how healthy it was.'

A picture of Dr KittyCat holding a long, thin dental probe with a sharp hook on the end popped into Peanut's mind. Had Dr KittyCat accidentally nicked Daisy's mouth with one of her dental instruments and made it sore?

Peanut gave a little *Eek!*

Dr KittyCat looked at him curiously. 'Is anything the matter, Peanut?' she asked. 'You're not panicking are you?'

'No, nothing's the matter,' Peanut squeaked. He took a deep breath. *Of course Dr KittyCat hasn't hurt Daisy*, he

told himself. *She's very well trained, and she's always so careful and gentle.*

Dr KittyCat opened her flowery doctor's bag and took out the little mirror on the long, thin handle.

'I want you to open your mouth wide,' she told Daisy, 'like you did at the Shiny Smiles clinic this morning.'

'I can't,' Daisy snuffled. 'It hurts too much,' she mumbled between clenched teeth. 'I heard you tell Bramble he didn't have to open his mouth unless he wanted to. Well, I wanted to this morning, but I don't want to now!'

'But I can only find out what's

wrong and make it better if you let me look inside your mouth,' Dr KittyCat explained. 'I promise I'll be very careful not to hurt you. Do you think you could try to open it a little?'

Daisy blinked her tear-filled eyes and reluctantly nodded her head.

'You are a brave kitten,' Dr KittyCat purred as Daisy slowly opened her mouth.

'What can you see?' Peanut asked anxiously

'I can't see very much at all,' Dr KittyCat meowed. 'I need a bit more light.'

Peanut reached into Dr KittyCat's

bag and took out her
surgical headlamp.
He helped her adjust
it and watched as Dr KittyCat very
carefully examined the inside of Daisy's
mouth with her dental mirror.

'I can't see anything seriously
wrong, and there's no swelling,'
Dr KittyCat reassured the little kitten.
'But your tongue and gums are very
pink.' She took off the headlamp and
handed it to Peanut to put away.

'My mouth is so sore!'
Daisy meowed.

Peanut flicked through
Dr KittyCat's *Furry First-aid Book*.

'Has Daisy got anything stuck between her teeth and gums, like the seed you removed from Nutmeg's mouth this morning?' he asked.

'I checked and I couldn't see anything like that,' Dr KittyCat told him. 'Daisy's teeth aren't as clean as they were. In fact, they're covered in cake crumbs, but cake wouldn't make her mouth sore . . .'

'Does she have any other symptoms?' Peanut asked.

Dr KittyCat looked Daisy over carefully.

'Her eyes are clear and bright, her ears are pricked, and her fur is smooth and glossy,' Dr KittyCat murmured. 'She doesn't look poorly at all.'

'Do you have a sore throat, Daisy?' she asked.

Daisy shook her head.

'Or a headache, or a sore tummy?' Again Daisy shook her head.

'Does anywhere else hurt at all, even a little bit?' Dr KittyCat asked.

Daisy paused before she spoke. 'My paws were sore a little while ago,' she meowed, 'but they feel better now.' She held out her front paws for Dr KittyCat to see.

'Hmm,' Dr KittyCat murmured. 'Your paw pads are a bit pink.'

'Eek!' Peanut squeaked in alarm. 'It's not pawpox is it?' There had recently been an outbreak of pawpox in Thistletown, but there hadn't been any new cases for a while.

'It can't be pawpox,' DrKittyCat said calmly. 'Daisy's already had that, remember?'

'Of course, you can't get it more than once,' Peanut sighed with relief.

'There is a rare illness called paw and mouth that causes pinkness in mouth and paws,' Dr KittyCat said thoughtfully

Peanut stifled another *Eek! I mustn't worry the patient*, he told himself.

'Paw and mouth is a very mild illness,' Dr KittyCat said reassuringly. 'So mild it is often missed. It causes a rise in the patient's body temperature along with the pink mouth and paws. I'll check to see if Daisy has a fever . . .'

Peanut took the ear thermometer out of Dr KittyCat's bag and fitted it

with a fresh hygiene cover before handing it to her.

'I'm just going to put this in your ear and hold it there until it beeps,' she told Daisy.

*Beep! Beep! Beep!*

Dr KittyCat examined the reading on the thermometer.

'Daisy's temperature is absolutely
normal for a kitten,' Dr KittyCat
declared. 'So she doesn't have paw
and mouth.'

*Then whatever is wrong with Daisy?*
Peanut wondered. He gazed round the

marquee at the little animals busily making and decorating their cup cakes. *Most of them are making eight cupcakes even though the competition is for six*, he thought. *That must be in case one or two*

*of the cakes go wrong and they have to*
*throw them away . . .*

'Oh!' Peanut squeaked. 'I think
I know what the matter is!'

# Chapter Four

'How many cupcakes did you bake?' Peanut gently questioned Daisy.

'Eight.' Daisy gave a little snuffle. 'All of them were purr-fect!'

'Did you wear oven gloves when you took them out of the oven?' Peanut went on.

'Yes!' Daisy meowed. 'That was

one of the rules. There are lots of rules.'

Peanut nodded thoughtfully. He
looked at the floor. There was a little
heap of crumbs in one spot.

'Did one of your cakes fall on the
floor?' Peanut squeaked.

Daisy nodded.

'Did you take off the oven gloves
to pick it up?' Peanut went on.

'Yes,' Daisy sniffed.

Peanut turned to Dr KittyCat. 'That explains why Daisy's paw pads are pink,' he murmured. Dr KittyCat nodded.

'Daisy, was that eighth cupcake still very hot when you tasted it?' Peanut asked the tiny kitten.

'Yes!' Daisy squeaked. 'I blew on it, but the toffee bits inside were still really hot,' she whispered.

'That explains everything,' Peanut sighed. 'You burned your paws and mouth by handling and eating a cup

cake while it was too hot. Why didn't
you tell us that straight away?'

Daisy hung her head. 'Because we
weren't supposed to eat any cupcakes
that fell on the floor,' she wailed. 'We
were supposed to throw them away.
I didn't want to get into trouble!'

'Mrs Hazelnut's much too busy to be cross with you,' Peanut squeaked comfortingly.

Dr KittyCat smiled. 'You worked everything out like a detective, Peanut. I'm very proud of you.'

*I'm proud of me, too,* thought Peanut.

'Now we know what's wrong, we can treat you, Daisy,' Dr KittyCat meowed.

'Your burns aren't serious. You should really have run your paws under cold water the instant you felt the burn, but never mind. Your paws are already getting better on their own, and the skin isn't broken, so they don't need any treatment . . .'

'But what about my mouth?' Daisy cried. 'It still hurts!'

'I can make that feel better straight away,' Dr KittyCat opened her flowery doctor's bag and took out a small tube. 'Here's some nice soothing gel that will work very quickly.'

Dr KittyCat squeezed a little mound of wobbly gel onto Daisy's paw and told her to rub it gently over her tongue and gums.

'Mmm,' Daisy murmured. 'That feels lovely and cool. And it tastes all minty fresh, like toothpaste.'

She gave a little purr. 'I feel much better now. I can carry on making the buttercream icing to decorate my cupcakes!'

Daisy poured icing sugar into a bowl and added a big lump of butter.

'You might need to rub a bit more gel onto your tongue and gums in an hour or so,' Dr KittyCat advised. She put the lid back on the tube of gel and handed it to Daisy.

'Thank you!' Daisy popped the gel into her apron pocket. Peanut couldn't

help smiling as the kitten held an
enormous wooden spoon between her
tiny paws and began to mix her butter
icing. A cloud of icing sugar flew into
the air.

*Ak . . . aak!* Daisy spluttered.

There was a surprised *Yip!* from
the counter next to hers. Peanut was
just in time to see Fennel almost drop
a tray of steaming cupcakes as he lifted
them from the oven.

'You made me jump, Daisy!' the
fox cub grumbled as he turned his

cupcakes onto a cooling rack and took
off his oven gloves.

‘Sorry, Fennel,’ Daisy meowed.
‘Some icing sugar got up my nose.
I’m really glad you didn’t burn yourself.
Burns hurt a lot!’

‘That was nearly a nasty accident,’
Peanut whispered to Dr KittyCat.

'And there's another accident waiting to happen . . .' Dr KittyCat pointed to the next bench along. Peanut followed her gaze. Posy the puppy was splattered from nose to tail with cake mix—and she had her nose almost pressed to the glass door of her oven.

Peanut hurried up to the sticky puppy.

'Posy, be careful! You'll burn your nose,' he squeaked anxiously. 'Your cupcakes will bake without you watching them!'

Posy took a step back and wagged her tail sheepishly. A glob of cake mix flew off her tail and caught Peanut on the ear.

*Splat!*

Mrs Hazelnut rushed over, looking worried.

'Mrs Hazelnut,' Dr KittyCat meowed. 'I think Peanut and I should stay just to keep an eye on Daisy, and

just in case there are any other mishaps with hot cakes.'

'Thank you!' Mrs Hazelnut exclaimed. 'It will be a while before all the cupcakes are finished for the judging session and I'm finding it hard to watch over everyone.'

'We'll be ready to rescue if you need us!' Peanut reassured her.

# Chapter
# Five

'This is the judging table.' Mrs Hazelnut led Peanut and Dr KittyCat to a round table covered in a checked tablecloth. 'Make yourselves comfortable,' she said, pulling out two chairs.

Peanut put Dr KittyCat's *Furry First-aid Book* down on the table and began to write up his notes on Daisy.

Dr KittyCat rummaged in her flowery doctor's bag and took out her knitting.

'This little hat I'm knitting will look really cute on you, Peanut,' she purred. 'I'll leave little holes for your ears . . .'

'Er . . . um . . . thanks, Dr KittyCat,' Peanut mumbled. He didn't like woolly hats, but how could he tell Dr KittyCat without hurting her feelings? He glanced up at the scene in the marquee. The little animals had

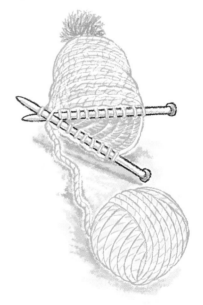

finished making their cupcakes and were busily cleaning up the mess with sponges, tea towels, and mops.

'Time to judge the cupcakes!' Mrs Hazelnut declared at last. 'Daisy, you're up first.'

Daisy proudly carried her cake stand of cupcakes to the table and set it down in front of Peanut and Dr KittyCat.

'I've made sticky toffee cupcakes with buttercream swirl,' she declared.

Peanut smiled. There was so much buttercream on the top of Daisy's cupcakes that they looked like upside down ice cream cones. And the little

kitten looked as if she'd been dusted
from nose to tail with icing sugar.

Peanut picked up a cupcake and
took a nibble. A big piece of toffee
came away in his mouth.

'Mrrm,' he mumbled. 'My teeth are stuck together!'

Dr KittyCat took a lick of buttercream.

'Delicious!' she exclaimed.

'Nutmeg next,' Mrs Hazelnut announced. 'Nutmeg's made seedy cupcakes with cherries on the top.'

Peanut sucked the toffee off his

teeth and took a big bite out of one of the guinea pig's cupcakes.

'That's my kind of cupcake,' he squeaked. 'Yum!'

'They're a bit dry for me,' Dr KittyCat said thoughtfully. She picked out a piece of seed from between her teeth. 'But they've given me an idea. If I put a little red bobble on the hat I'm knitting, you will look just like one of Nutmeg's cherry cupcakes when you're wearing it!'

Peanut shuddered. 'I think you should give the hat to Nutmeg,' he suggested hurriedly. 'I wouldn't mind at all.'

'That's a lovely idea,' Dr KittyCat meowed.

Peanut breathed a sigh of relief as the next contestant came up to the table.

'I've put lots of sprinkles on my cupcakes,' Posy woofed.

'I can see that.' Peanut looked at the sticky puppy and chuckled. 'There are lots of sprinkles stuck to your fur, too.'

'Posy's cupcakes look a little messy,' Dr KittyCat commented. 'But they are nice and light and moist.'

'The flavour's very good, too,' mumbled Peanut, with his mouth full of crumbs.

'Don't eat too much of each cupcake,' Dr KittyCat warned him. 'There are cupcakes from five other young bakers to go . . .'

At last, Peanut and Dr KittyCat had tasted all the cupcakes. Cupcakes with buttercream, cupcakes with sprinkles, cupcakes with smiley faces, seedy cupcakes, crunchy nut cupcakes, butterfly cupcakes with fondant icing, honeycomb cupcakes and, finally, Willow the duckling's white chocolate cupcakes. Peanut wasn't sure he ever wanted to see another cupcake.

'Who do you think should be the winner?' Dr KittyCat asked Peanut.

'It's too hard to choose,' Peanut said. 'Some looked a lot better than they tasted and others tasted a lot better than they looked. I liked the taste of the seedy and nutty ones best.'

'And I liked the ones with buttercream,' Dr KittyCat laughed. 'I think the fairest thing is to call it a draw.'

'That's a great idea,' Peanut squeaked.

Dr KittyCat stood up. 'You have all made brilliant cupcakes,' she declared. 'Peanut and I have found it very, very hard to choose the winner. But after a lot of discussion, we have made our decision. The winner is . . .'

She paused. Silence
fell on the marquee.
Peanut smiled—all the
little animals looked as if
they were holding their breath . . .

'EVERYONE!'

'Woo hoo!' all the little animals
jumped up and down and cheered
as Peanut handed out 'Cupcake Bake
Winner' badges to everyone.

'And now,' Dr KittyCat
announced, 'it's time to eat up the
cupcakes!'

The marquee filled with the sound
of little animals nibbling and chomping.

'Time to go!' Peanut squeaked. Dr KittyCat picked up her bag and put it on the table.

'I'll be ready in a whisker. I just need to put my knitting away . . .' she meowed.

Daisy hurried up to them. She handed Dr KittyCat a small package wrapped in greaseproof paper.

'I saved you a cupcake each to thank you very much for making me feel better today,' she told them.

'Thank you, Daisy,' Dr KittyCat purred. 'We'll save them for later, won't we, Peanut?'

Peanut nodded.

'My tummy is really full right now,' he squeaked.

I was a purr-fect patient for Dr KittyCat!

Dr KittyCat opened her bag and put her knitting and Daisy's present inside.

'You were so busy decorating your cupcakes, I forgot to give you a sticker,' she told Daisy. 'Would you like one?'

'Yes, please!' Daisy's eyes lit up as Dr KittyCat handed her a sticker which said: 'I was a purr-fect patient for Dr KittyCat!'

'Uh-oh,' Peanut squeaked. 'I think we have another patient.'

Fennel was making his way to their
table with his tail between his legs.
'Dr KittyCat,' he groaned, 'I've eaten
too many cupcakes and I feel a bit sick.'

'I have just the thing for that.'
Dr KittyCat delved into her bag and
took out a little box.

'Suck on this peppermint lozenge,' she told Fennel. 'It will settle your tummy in no time at all.'

'Thank you,' Fennel yipped. 'Please may I have a sticker like Daisy's?'

'Of course!' Dr KittyCat said, and she handed him one.

Soon there was a line of little animals all asking for peppermint lozenges and stickers. There were just enough to go round.

'It was hard to tell who had eaten too many cupcakes and who just wanted a sticker,' Dr KittyCat meowed as they made their way back to the vanbulance.

'Everyone wanted one of your stickers,' Peanut smiled, 'but I think they'd all eaten too many cupcakes, as well.'

'You ate a lot of cupcakes, too,' Dr KittyCat said. 'How are you feeling?'

'Fine!' Peanut squeaked as he jumped into the vanbulance. 'How about you?'

Dr KittyCat said nothing, but smiled at Peanut uncertainly.

# Chapter Six

The vanbulance chugged down the narrow lane through Thistletown

    'You're driving much more slowly than usual,' Peanut commented.

    'There's no hurry on the way back,' Dr KittyCat meowed. 'It's good to take it easy.'

She pressed one paw to her mouth. Her whiskers twitched.

'Are you feeling ok?' Peanut asked as Dr KittyCat carefully steered the vanbulance around Duckpond Bend.

Dr KittyCat cleared her throat.

'My tummy does feel a little wobbly,' she confessed. 'But maybe it's just the bumps in the road and nothing to do with the cupcakes.'

Peanut wasn't sure he believed her. He didn't want to admit it, but he was beginning to feel a little bit sick himself. He swallowed hard as the vanbulance bumped slowly over the timber bridge and rumbled to a halt outside Dr KittyCat's clinic.

It was time to pack up the Shiny Smiles equipment. Peanut slowly folded away the screen and wheeled the dentist's chair into the corner.

'It's been another busy day,'
Peanut squeaked. 'We saw an awful lot
of patients.'

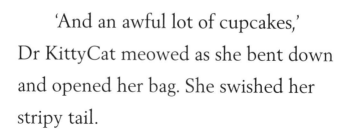

'And an awful lot of cupcakes,' Dr KittyCat meowed as she bent down and opened her bag. She swished her stripy tail.

'More cupcakes,' she groaned, holding up Daisy's present. 'Do you want one, Peanut?'

'I'll save it for tomorrow,' Peanut told Dr KittyCat. 'Right now, I would like one of your peppermint lozenges instead!'

'That's a very good idea,' Dr KittyCat meowed. 'There's a new box of lozenges in the supplies cupboard. I think I'll have one, too.'

Peanut and Dr KittyCat sat down

in their chairs and sucked on their peppermint lozenges.

'That's better,' Peanut sighed.

Dr KittyCat took her knitting out of her bag.

'You did really well today,' Dr KittyCat told Peanut, as she clicked away with her knitting needles. 'For a while I was puzzled about what was wrong with Daisy.'

'I was puzzled, too,' Peanut admitted, 'until I counted her cupcakes.'

'I'd hate to count how many cupcakes we tasted today,' Dr KittyCat murmured.

'At least eight each,' Peanut told her.

'That's far too much sugar for one day,' Dr KittyCat declared. 'It's the main cause of dental decay.'

'Eek!' Peanut squeaked. 'I don't want my teeth to fall out!'

'Don't panic, Peanut,' Dr KittyCat told him. 'Your teeth won't fall out if you clean them carefully.'

Peanut jumped to his feet. 'I'm going to brush my teeth NOW,' he squeaked.

Dr KittyCat put down her knitting. 'So am I,' she meowed. 'And that way, we'll both keep our shiny smiles!'

The end

# What's in Dr KittyCat's bag?

Here are just some of the things that Dr KittyCat always carries in her flowery doctor's bag.

## Dental mirror

Dr KittyCat uses her dental mirror to examine her patients' teeth and gums. She finds its long thin handle very useful, as it helps her to see right to the back of her patients' mouths.

## Cooling gel

When her patients have sore mouths, Dr KittyCat tells them to gently rub a little bit of cooling gel over the area where it hurts. The gel stops the swelling and soothes the pain. It also contains antiseptic, which stops infection and speeds up the healing process.

## Sticking plasters

Plasters are sticky strips of
material used for covering
up cuts and scrapes, to protect
the wound and make sure that dirt
doesn't get inside. They come with
all sorts of patterns, including
stars and butterflies, but Peanut's
favourites are the plasters covered
in little paw prints.

## Peppermint lozenges

Peppermint lozenges are excellent
for settling upset tummies. Dr
KittyCat always carries some
lozenges in her bag for those times
when she gets that 'too full up'
feeling, because she knows that
peppermint relaxes the muscles in
the tummy.

If you loved Daisy the Kitten, here's an extract
from another Dr KittyCat adventure:

# Dr KittyCat is ready to rescue: Posy the Puppy

This time Dr KittyCat is helping a little puppy
called Posy who's worried she won't be well enough
to take part in the Paws and Prizes sports day . . .

'I . . . I chewed up one of your
things!' Posy lifted her head and looked Dr
KittyCat in the eye. 'I tried to spit it out,
but I couldn't—and I couldn't swallow it,
either. I haven't been able to eat anything
since then and I'm *so* hungry . . .'

'Hunger pangs can be very painful,'
Peanut said sympathetically. 'That would
explain why your tummy hurts.'

'We need to check out why you can't swallow,' Dr KittyCat meowed. 'I'll have to look down your throat, Posy. Open wide . . .'

# Here are some other stories that we think you'll love!